THE CAPTIVE CELT

THE CAPTIVE CELT

Illustrated by Helen Flook

A & C Black • London

First published 2008 by
A & C Black Publishers Ltd
38 Soho Square, London, W1D 3HB

www.acblack.com

ISBN 978-0-7136-8960-0

A CIP catalogue for this book is available from the British Library.

This book is produced using paper that is made from wood grown in
managed, sustainable forests. It is natural, renewable and recyclable.
The logging and manufacturing processes conform to the
environmental regulations of the country of origin.

Printed and bound in Great Britain by Cox & Wyman Ltd.

ONE

Rome, AD 51

I am a slave. A pitiful, helpless boy, bullied by my master the senator's daughter, the cruel Livia.

I am a prisoner of Rome.

There is no winter in Rome ...
not real winter like in Britannia,
my home. And it was winter that
defeated us, not just the Roman
army. Winter and the shortest day
of the year.

I remember what my father said.
"The days are getting shorter – the
sun is getting weaker. It happens
every year. The grass will not grow
and we will starve."

"How can we make the sun stronger?" I asked.

"Give the gods a gift."

"A gift?"

"A life."

"A goat?" I had seen a goat sacrificed to the gods. The druids took their knives and cut its throat. They roasted the meat and ate it. I was given some of the scraps.

But this year, it would not be a goat.

"A man," my father said.

"The Roman soldier? The one we captured?"

Father nodded.

The druids would never roast or eat a man. But they *would* kill him and give his life to our gods.

The whole village gathered on the path that led to the woods. The five druid priests in their white robes stood silent and still, though a wicked wind whipped at their hoods and blew through their beards.

The dark-skinned Roman soldier looked at us with scorn. He was not afraid to die.

TWO

The druids turned and walked
slowly up the hill to the dark, bare
trees. Our warriors led the way,
guarding the prisoner.
Children like me
followed.

I tried to march like a warrior, but my little feet slipped in the muddy puddles. The only sound was the sighing of the wind in the trees and the crying of some of the babies the women carried.

"Why are you wearing your black war dress, Ma?" I asked.

"For luck," she said. "This was the dress I was wearing when we attacked the Roman supply wagon."

"Was that when we stole their corn?" I asked.

My mother nodded. "We ate well that night," she said with a grim smile.

The druids stopped beneath a huge oak tree. The soldier was tied to a rough table raised on a bank of earth – the druid altar.

I watched wide-eyed and dry-mouthed for the knives to slice and the guts to spill. They said the druids could see the future from the way the guts fell to the ground.

But they hadn't seen the future that day. They hadn't seen what would happen next. They hadn't even guessed there would be a Roman revenge.

As the druids raised their knives, there was a single cry in a strange tongue. Then came a crashing of branches and ferns as a troop of Roman soldiers rose from their hiding places and raced towards us. They carried no shields, only throwing spears and short swords.

Our warriors carried no weapons
– they would never do that on
holy ground. One of the first spears
struck my mother. She fell and
dropped my baby sister to the
ground.

Smiling, she said, "I will see you
again, son, when I am reborn."
Then the light of this life went out
of her eyes and she slipped into
the next.

My mother was not afraid to die.

I pulled the spear from her chest and tried to fling it back, but the point had snapped off ... the Romans made them that way.

Sweeping swords spilled blood as our warriors died bravely. The women who tried to fight were cut down without mercy. Children who tried to run were beaten back.

I didn't see my father die, but all the men were killed. The white druid robes were stained red.

In moments, the clearing in the woods was almost silent again. A few of the dying groaned. Some children sobbed. I watched as the prisoner was cut free and hugged his fellow Romans.

A soldier grabbed me roughly by
the shoulder and raised his sword.

I waited to die. He spoke the foreign
tongue to a friend. They looked at
me, shrugged and the Roman said,
"Servus."

I soon learned that meant slave.

I was chained to the few children who were left. The ones who were old enough to fight were killed. The ones who were too young to walk were killed.

We were marched for many days to the edge of the ocean. There we were led on to boats.

The winter sea was wild. I looked back through the spray at the white cliffs. They were the first sight many Romans had of Britannia, so they called our country "Albion", which means white. It was *my* last sight of my homeland for many years...

THREE

It was a holiday in Rome. The streets were filled with bakers and butchers and builders, muck movers and

moneylenders and metalworkers,
soldiers and sewer men and
swineherds, cowherds and cooks
and crooks, potters and pedlars
and even priests.

They came like an invading army,
bubbling along in a loud and
swirling stream towards the Circus
Maximus and the chariot races.

There were snarling race fans with their green, red, blue or white ribbons. There were grand men in togas, who sniffed at the stinking mob while slaves flapped fans and pushed beggars out of the way and back to the gutters.

Then there was me ... Deri the Brave, the young Celtic warrior. And there was the girl. The ugly, raven-haired, sour-faced, spoilt brat they call Livia.

She squawked in her whining way, "That beggar woman trod on my toe!"

"So?" I shrugged.

"So, Father sent you along to protect me." Her too-fat face turned red and she roared, "You are a slave, you uncaring Celt. You do as I say."

"I do as your father, my master, says," I argued.

"And my father told you that today you would protect me. So protect me."

"What do you want me to do?"

"Take your stick and beat that woman who trampled on my toe!"

"Which woman?" I asked.

The crowd had swirled on and the figures and faces had shifted like shapes in the clouds on a windy day.

We had clouds like that back in Britannia. I would lie on my back and watch them change. I would see animals and monsters come and melt away.

Here in Rome, they had endless days of clear, blue sky.

In Britannia, we had fields and
forests of fifty shades of green,
morning skies of lemon and amber,
and evening skies of scarlet and
pink. Britannia had the colours of
the rainbow. Rome had the colours
of mud.

"Ha!" limp-haired Livia jeered. "Call yourself a warrior! What warrior sheds tears because a girl shouts at him?"

If a tear ran down my face, it was not because of Livia. It was the memory of Britannia that was hurting my heart.

I brushed it away. The slave collar burned my neck and I longed to be free of it.

One day my life will change, I thought. I know it will.

FOUR

"No wonder the Romans defeated you Celts when you cry like girls," Livia sneered.

"They cheat – the Romans cheat!" I raged. "They hide in the woods and kill our warriors on holy ground!"

The noisy crowds stopped to look at me, a slave, standing on the dusty street, shouting at a noble girl. They probably wanted to see me executed for my cheek – the Romans love to watch a good execution.

I bit my lip to stop my ranting and breathed deeply. I walked on towards the large wooden stadium, the Circus Maximus.

"The Romans took us by surprise," I told her, more quietly. "They would never have beaten us in open battle. It was Midwinter's Day and we were going to the holy wood to make our sacrifice."

"Ha!" Livia laughed bitterly. "Human sacrifices. Yes, I've heard your priests do that. We kill goats and lambs, and offer them to our gods. But *you* kill humans. That's why you have to be defeated. The Romans are saving the world from barbarians like you."

"But you kill people for fun!" I spat. "You have your games, where men and women are torn apart by lions and bears, where they're made to fight to the death, just for sport. You're evil ... all of you Romans. Evil!"

I felt better for saying that. But a crowd was gathering close by. A group of men had made a circle around me. They had no weapons, but their huge fists and boots could easily crush me.

"What do we do with slaves that rebel?" a fat one burbled.

"Beat them till they've learned their lesson," his friend hissed.

There was no escape – the crowd
was packed too tightly. I was ready
to die.

But then a soldier pushed his
way through the mob and raised
his sword. "That's enough,"
he snarled.

"We have Roman law to deal with this – you can't defeat the barbarians by acting like barbarians."

The men nodded, and began to move away. Only Livia stood there, red faced and furious. "What will you do to him?" she screeched.

"What we do with all rebel slaves," the man shrugged. "Crucify him. Fasten him to a cross by the side of the road into Rome. Leave him to die slowly. Show the world what happens to animals like him."

"Good," Livia snorted and walked away.

"Thanks, officer," I muttered.

FIVE

I was taken to the camp of the emperor's guard in the centre of Rome. I'd been past the gates many times, and seen the troops marching and training. These were men who fought and beat the rest of the world.

As it was a holiday, today there was no training. Captains and generals with high plumes on their helmets rode on horses. They galloped through the gates, as excited as children playing in the streets.

I was sure I was on my way to a slow death, but I had to ask: "What's going on?"

The soldier grunted. "A special prisoner's just been brought to Rome. There will be a great parade to show him to the people. It will be more popular than the chariot races."

We passed guards who unlocked gates and doors for us until we reached a block of cells. They stank like Roman toilet rooms in summer – the ones I had to clean out.

At last, a heavy door was opened
and I was thrown into a dark room.
I stumbled and crashed into
someone who was already there.

He steadied me with his huge
hands and said, "Careful, boy!" And
he wasn't speaking Latin like the
Romans. He wasn't even a Gaul.

My heart seemed to stop for a
moment. "You're from Britannia!"

There was a tiny window in the top of the cell to let in air and a little light. As my eyes grew used to the dimness, I could see he was a tall man, dressed like a British warrior though they'd taken away his weapons. "I'm Deri," I said.

"They're going to execute me for being a rebel slave."

"Ah, that's the Roman way," the man nodded. "I am a British chief ... and they're going to execute me for daring to fight them. My name is Caratacus."

SIX

This time I was sure my heart wouldn't start beating again. "Caratacus? The mighty chief? My father told me about your amazing deeds. You are the greatest hero Britannia has ever seen. You are a god ... they could never capture you, my lord!"

The man chuckled softly. "Not in battle, no. But the Romans have other ways. And I was a fool."

"No, you're a hero," I argued. "The Celtic leader of leaders!"

"A warrior can be a hero and a
fool, Deri. When Emperor Claudius
invaded Britannia ten years ago,
I led the tribes who wanted to fight.
But they defeated us time and again.
Of course, some tribes welcomed
the Romans and fought for them.
Maybe we should have made peace
like the cowards. But we did not.
They drove us west till I ended in
the land of Wales."

"And you led the Welsh into great battles. You were a hero there, too," I reminded him.

"Not really. I robbed a few Roman supply wagons. But when it came to battles, they beat us again. Finally, after years of fighting, we fled to a fortress on a cliff top in the Welsh mountains. From there, we could pour stones on to their heads if they tried to attack us," he told me.

"So you beat them in the end?"

"No. They put those great curved shields over their heads to make a roof ... they call it a 'tortoise' ... and they marched on us till they captured the fort.

"I was lucky. I escaped. But they took my family. I didn't know what to do, so I went over to the Brigantes in northern England for help."

"The Brigantes?" I gasped. "But I've heard that they are friends with the Romans ... they are traitors! They make peace and the Romans protect them. Their queen Cartimandua is a witch!"

Caratacus snorted. "I know that *now*. But I believed she was a true Celt at heart. When I arrived at her fortress, she welcomed me as a friend. Then, that evening, she drugged my wine and when I woke I was in chains and a prisoner of the Romans."

"The Iceni tribe would never have betrayed you. Queen Boudica will fight to the end. I wish I was back in Britannia to fight with her. Instead, I'll die in Rome," I said.

Caratacus wrapped a powerful arm around my shoulders. "You will die bravely like a Celt. I'll show you how."

My mouth was dry with fear, but I knew I mustn't show it. I would show the evil Livia how a Briton could die ... I knew she'd be there to watch.

The guard brought us some dry bread and slimy water.

"When do we die?" I asked.

"Tomorrow," he said and bolted the door shut.

"You speak the Latin tongue?" Caratacus was surprised.

"I've been here five years," I said. "I had to learn it."

"What did the guard say?"

"We die tomorrow," I said, and we sank into silence.

Night fell. We slept.

SEVEN

We were woken by the sound of
trumpets from the exercise yard
outside our window. There was a lot
·of clattering – armour and arms,
horses and chariots, and centurions
in hob-nailed sandals shouting
orders.

We were led out, blinking, into the light and saw a glittering line of troops ready to march out of the camp gates. A chariot stood at the back of the line, and Caratacus was made to climb into it, with his wrists and ankles chained. Of course a slave boy like me had to walk behind.

A trumpet rang out and the line moved forward. It was a fine morning to die.

When we entered the street, the crowds were thick. The guards had trouble holding them back. Some wine-filled peasants tried to throw stones, but most just jeered and laughed at the fallen hero.

We reached the great meeting place in the middle of Rome – the Forum – but instead of heading for the arena and the wild animals, we were led to the senate building.

I'd never been inside, but I knew that was where the nobles of Rome met to make their laws and plot their wars. Were they planning to kill us in front of the lords?

Caratacus was taken from the chariot and led into the cool, marble hall, where a hundred men in brilliant-white togas stared at him in silence. He leaned towards me. "Tell them I need you – a warrior lord must have his weapon carrier."

I nodded and passed on the message in Latin. The guards looked at the brave figure of Caratacus and didn't argue.

The families of the great men crowded in behind us. Then someone stepped forward – a beetle-backed man with a limp and an ugly face. "Welcome to Rome, Caratacus," he said.

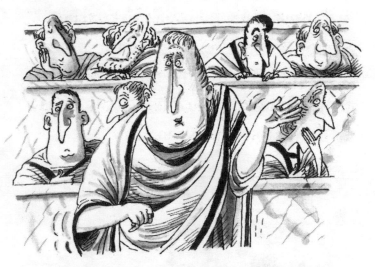

Caratacus turned and looked at me. "What did he say?"

"It's the emperor Claudius, and he welcomed you," I explained.

"Tell him I wish to speak to the nobles of Rome."

"But you don't speak Latin," I said.

"*You* do. I'll tell you what to say. I need to try to argue for my life," he murmured.

"Are you afraid to die?" I asked, shocked.

"No, but I don't want to see a kind friend like you die, Deri. Now, speak to the emperor for me."

EIGHT

Caratacus told me what to say.
Many years later, the writer Tacitus
put the great speech in a book. But
the words came from *my* lips. As
Caratacus spoke, I changed the
words into Latin.

"I am a great lord in Britannia.
If I had been greater in battle, I
would be here now as a friend not a
prisoner. I would have come here in
peace. But I stand here in disgrace,
and you stand here in glory. I had
horses, men, arms, and wealth; you

cannot blame me if I fought to keep them. Not all beaten people wish to be your slaves. If I had just given in, you would not have had any glory. Now, you have defeated a hero."

The great senators of Rome muttered as if they agreed. Then Caratacus said something as mad as it was daring.

"If you keep me alive, then all the world will see how great I was ... and how great Rome must be to capture me!"

There was silence. Then the ugly little emperor laughed aloud. The lords joined in and then began to clap and cheer.

"A brave speech, Caratacus. And it's true what you say. We will let you live. We will give you a house in Rome and the sort of wealth you are used to."

I told Caratacus what the emperor had said and he gave his reply. "I want just one thing, Emperor Claudius ... I want this boy Deri as my slave."

My heart swelled so large I swear it choked my throat and made my eyes water.

"No!" came the shrill voice of a girl from the back of the senate. "He insulted me – he insulted Rome – he must die!"

It was the cruel Livia.

The emperor frowned at the senator, Livia's father. "Take the child home and give her a good whipping," he ordered.

My master ... my old master ... bowed quickly and hurried off to take the raging girl home.

My new master, Caratacus, took
me to the mansion the Romans
gave him.

So was I still a slave?

No. Caratacus didn't treat me as
a servant, but as a son. He taught
me all the skills of fighting that
had made him such a great warrior.
I learned quickly.

Then, three years later, when I was
older and stronger, Caratacus let me
slip away one night and take the
road back to Britannia. My master
was lost to the fight for freedom,
but I could carry it on.

One day, Boudica and our Iceni
will rise up and carry on the fight
against the Roman enemies. We will
never give in. Never.

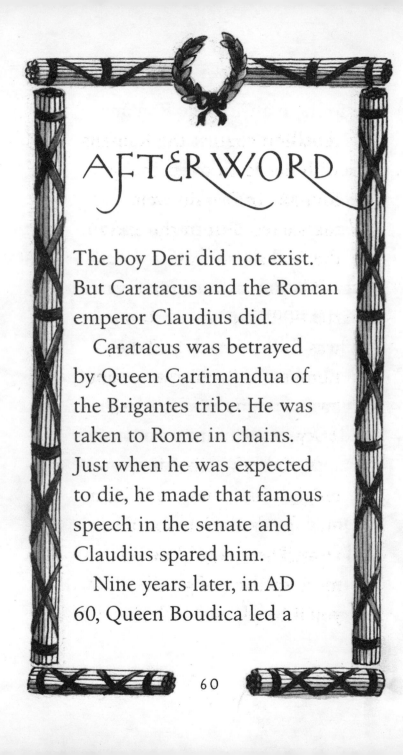

AFTERWORD

The boy Deri did not exist.
But Caratacus and the Roman
emperor Claudius did.

Caratacus was betrayed
by Queen Cartimandua of
the Brigantes tribe. He was
taken to Rome in chains.
Just when he was expected
to die, he made that famous
speech in the senate and
Claudius spared him.

Nine years later, in AD
60, Queen Boudica led a

rebellion against the Romans with her Iceni tribe. Many Romans in Britain were massacred. But in the end the Romans won.

They stayed until about AD 409. The city of Rome was under attack and the Romans in Britain were sent back to fight for their city. They never returned.

By then the Christian religion had come to Britain, and the druid religion died away. There would be no more spilling of guts ... you'll be pleased to hear!

ROME, 387 BC

The cruel Gauls are attacking Rome.
High on the Capitol Hill, the priests have been
defending the temple of Juno for weeks. But food
is running out and their only hope of help is from
the army of Lord Furius. Will he arrive in time?
And what will they do if he doesn't?

Roman Tales are exciting, funny stories based
on historical events - short chapters and
illustrations throughout are perfect for
building reading confidence.

ISBN 978 0 7136 8963 1   £4.99

ROME, AD 64

Rome is a dangerous place. Especially on the
day of the chariot races, and for a young girl.
When Mary finds herself the only witness to
a terrible crime, soon it is not just the thieves
and drunks that she has to worry about, but
someone far more cruel and powerful...

Roman Tales are exciting, funny stories based
on historical events - short chapters and
illustrations throughout are perfect for
building reading confidence.

ISBN 978 0 7136 8970 9   £4.99

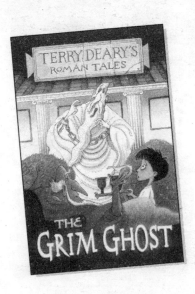

ROME, AD 113

Pertinax is helping prepare magnificent
dishes for a feast to be held by the great
lawyer Pliny. While the boy is working,
Pliny tells him the story of a terrifying ghost
who haunted a garden not unlike Pliny's own.
But there's no truth in ghost stories ... is there?

Roman Tales are exciting, funny stories based
on historical events - short chapters and
illustrations throughout are perfect for
building reading confidence.

ISBN 978 0 7136 8961 7   £4.99